To our family: Let's go to the beach! —LMK & KHM

A nuestra familia: ¡Vamos a la playa! —LMK y KHM

PHILOMEL BOOKS

An imprint of Penguin Random House LLC, New York

First published in the United States of America by Philomel,
an imprint of Penguin Random House LLC, 2021

Text copyright © 2021 by Laura McGee Kvasnosky
Translation copyright © 2022 by Penguin Random House LLC
Illustrations copyright © 2021 by Laura McGee Kvasnosky and Kate Harvey McGee

Visit us online at penguinrandomhouse.com.

Library of Congress Control Number: 2021933941

Manufactured in China

ISBN 9780593118016 (hardcover)

Special Markets ISBN 9780593527382

Not for resale

10 9 8 7 6 5 4 3

RRD

Edited by Talia Benamy.
Design by Monique Sterling.
Text set in Adderville.

With thanks to marine science teacher Susan Barth.

This Imagination Library edition is published by Penguin Young Readers, a division of Penguin Random House LLC, exclusively for Dolly Parton's Imagination Library, a not-for-profit program designed to inspire a love of reading and learning, sponsored in part by The Dollywood Foundation. Penguin's trade editions of this work are available wherever books are sold.

Ocean Lullaby
El arrullo del océano

Laura McGee Kvasnosky

Kate Harvey McGee

Traducido por Eva Ibarzábal

PHILOMEL BOOKS

Song floats up, moon smiles down,
while we rock to ocean sounds.

Una canción se eleva y hace sonreír a la luna
mientras el rítmico sonido del mar nos acuna.

Shhh, hush. Shhh, hush. The ocean's soothing song.

Shhh, shhh . . . shhhhh. Escucha la melodía del mar.

Shhh, hush. Shhh, hush. We can sing along.

Shhh, shhh . . . shhhhh. Vamos a coro todos a cantar.

Far offshore the big whales doze.
Moms nudge calves to keep them close.

Lejos de la orilla, las grandes ballenas dormitan a ratos;
las madres impulsan y mantienen cerca a sus ballenatos.

Turtles float and shut their eyes.
Jellies undulate and rise.

Las tortugas flotan y a sus anchas duermen
y las aguas vivas ondeando emergen.

Shhh, hush. Shhh, hush. The ocean's soothing song.
Shhh, shhh . . . shhhhh. Escucha la melodía del mar.

Dolphins drift and mantas glide
through the rocking, rolling tide.

Mantarrayas y delfines se deslizan y planean
Bamboleando al compás de la ondulante marea.

Along the reef, fish hide and spread,
tucked into their coral bed.

Los peces, resguardados en su cama de coral,
hallan en el arrecife el escondite ideal.

Shhh, hush. Shhh, hush. We can sing along.
Shhh, shhh . . . shhhhh. Vamos a coro todos a cantar.

Octopus dreams in her cave
underneath the swelling waves.

El pulpo duerme en su cueva aislada
debajo de la intensa marejada.

Tide pools catch the moonlight's glow.
Stars above, sea stars below.

Las pozas reflejan el resplandor lunar.
Estrellas en el cielo, estrellas en el mar.

Shhh, hush. Shhh, hush. The ocean's soothing song.

Shhh, shhh . . . shhhhh. Escucha la melodía del mar.

Monk seals find a sandy shore,
stretch their flippers, start to snore.

Las focas monje a la playa llegan,
estiran sus aletas y a roncar se entregan.

Rising waves break, spill and reach,
smoothing footsteps from the beach.

Las olas rompen y arriban serenas
hasta borrar las huellas en la arena.

Shhh, hush. Shhh, hush. We can sing along.
Shhh, shhh . . . shhhhh. Vamos a coro todos a cantar.

You, my sweet, my sleepy child,
rest here in my arms awhile.
As the new moon rides the sky,
dream the ocean lullaby.

Mi dulce niño que el sueño doblega,
ven a mis brazos a descansar.
Mientras la luna por los cielos navega,
sueña tú con el arrullo del mar.

Shhh, hush. Shhh, hush.
Shhh, shhh . . . shhhhh.